STAR WARS
ROGUE ONE™

REBEL DOSSIER

INFO & INTEL ON THE REBELLION'S BRAVEST BAND OF SPIES

BY JASON FRY

Printed in the United States of America

First Edition, December 2016

1 3 5 7 9 10 8 6 4 2

Library of Congress Control Number on file

FAC-038091-16309

ISBN 978-1-4847-8079-4

Imperial propaganda poster art by Russell Walks

VISIT THE OFFICIAL *STAR WARS* WEBSITE AT: WWW.STARWARS.COM.

Disney

LUCASFILM
PRESS

FROM

GEN. AIREN CRACKEN,
CHIEF OF REBEL INTELLIGENCE

TO

MON MOTHMA,
COMMANDER IN CHIEF OF THE
ALLIANCE

As requested, I have prepared this dossier about the rumored Imperial weapons test and KEY PERSONNEL involved in Operation Fracture.

Many of these documents will be familiar, but I thought gathering them in one place would be helpful in these trying times. I've included the following:

Documents you requested before we learned of the Empire's weapons test

Intelligence briefings about our team and the enemies they may encounter

Discussions of what the Imperial weapon may be

Profiles of key Imperial personnel and military units

The Empire's weapons test threatens all we have created in resisting the Emperor's rule.

May the Force be with you, Commander—and with all of us.

Bail Organa
Former senator of Alderaan

General Dodonna
Republic Military

General Draven
Rebel Intelligence

Admiral Raddus
Rebel Navy

THE STATE OF THE REBELLION

 BAIL ORGANA TO COMMANDER MOTHMA

You asked me for my thoughts on the state of our rebel movement against the Empire. To be honest, we are in serious trouble.

We lack the military power to stand up to the Empire in an all-out fight. We can't match the Empire's growing network of military bases, garrisons, and space stations, but we have our own secret bases spread across the galaxy that give our forces safe places to train and rest. The galaxy is enormous, and we have used that fact to successfully stay hidden.

The Empire's own relentless expansion has helped us in some ways. Sympathetic senators have arranged for warships built for the Empire to go missing and wind up in rebel hands—a trick I'm proud to say I taught my daughter, Leia, before she took over my duties as Alderaan's senator. Planets such as Mon Cala have donated warships to our cause, in defiance of the Empire. And we have acquired weapons, vehicles, and starfighters left on the battlefields of the Clone Wars.

Our military strength, while small compared with that of the Empire, is far better than it was just a few years ago.

IMAGE CELL 0004

IMAGE CELL 0005

But military strength isn't everything.

The Empire is our most fearsome enemy, but it is not our only enemy. Simply put, we are at war with ourselves.

IMAGE CELL 0006

The galaxy's many rebel movements are all led by brave beings who oppose the Empire. But that's about the only thing on which they agree. We are sharply divided on everything else: What tactics should we use against the Empire? Which Imperial facilities should we target? What's our ultimate goal?

Some of us believe we should negotiate with the Emperor. Others say we must fight for our lives. Some of us believe we can win victories with bombings and bombardments on Imperial worlds. Others warn that will just increase support for Palpatine.

I no longer think talking can bring us together. We need something to unite all these rebel movements so they become a true alliance. Until that happens, we will remain divided—and dangerously weak.

THE STATE OF THE EMPIRE

 ADVISER HOSTIS IJ TO COMMANDER MOTHMA

The Empire continues to expand, building new warships, recruiting new stormtroopers, and taking over new planets. Every day we learn of a new atrocity committed by the Empire against its own citizens.

The Emperor is surrounded by advisers who tell him only what they think he wants to hear. His orders are carried out by governors, moffs, and grand moffs who have been appointed to rule planets and whole regions of space in his name.

The only piece of the Republic that still exists is the Imperial Senate. In the Senate, the voice of the people is still heard, and a few brave senators still defy the Emperor. But the Senate has little power. Most of that now belongs to Palpatine's governors and the Imperial bureaucracy.

Commander, I know you believe the Senate can still protect the people of the galaxy from the Emperor and his henchmen.

But as your adviser, it is my duty to tell you that I no longer believe this. With respect, ma'am, the Senate could not protect you. Yours was the most passionate voice to speak up against Palpatine, and you had to flee for your life or face imprisonment and execution. We have few allies left in the Senate, Commander, and they will soon face the same terrible choice you did: escape or die.

The only thing we can do is fight.

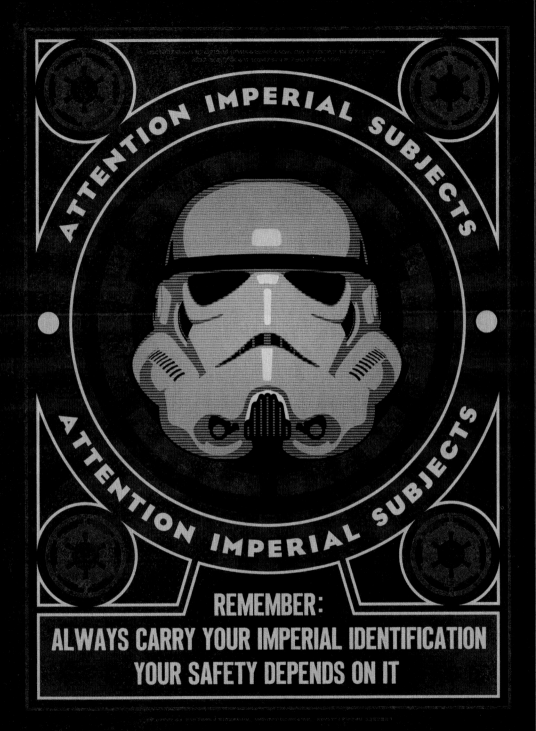

ATTENTION IMPERIAL SUBJECTS

ATTENTION IMPERIAL SUBJECTS

REMEMBER:
ALWAYS CARRY YOUR IMPERIAL IDENTIFICATION
YOUR SAFETY DEPENDS ON IT

IMAGE CELL 0007

THE STATE OF THE GALAXY

Twenty years ago, the galaxy was at war. People lived in fear that fighting would come to their planet or that a terrorist attack would strike near their home. For Republic citizens, seeing white-armored troopers and warships overhead meant they were safe. Today, people who remember those dark days see the arrival of stormtroopers and Imperial Star Destroyers the same way.

Many galactic citizens also remember the time before **PALPATINE** became Supreme Chancellor. They remember that the Republic was corrupt and weak, with slavers and pirates attacking travelers and taking over planets on the frontier. They remember that powerful corporations controlled the Senate and the courts, so ordinary people had no hope of getting justice. Many of those citizens think the Empire ended corruption. They approve of the Emperor as a strong leader who has made sacrifices for the good of the galaxy and survived assassination attempts.

IMAGE CELL 0008

TRANSMISSION
INCOMPLETE
ID 345-A002

IMAGE CELL 0009

Frankly, we have little hope of reaching citizens who believe these things. The best thing we can do is remind the others that we are not Separatists but beings who believe in restoring the Republic and making it work better for all citizens.

And our actions must show people that we are at war with the Empire, not Imperial civilians. If we succeed, our cause will continue to gain support in the Senate and more citizens will ask whether order and security are worth sacrificing basic freedoms.

THE ERSO LINK

Gen. Cracken,

As ordered, I have been investigating reports that the Empire is transporting kyber crystals to Patriim, Horuz, and other remote star systems. Those investigations led me to Corulag and then to Coruscant, where I heard rumors that the Empire was concealing shipments of kyber crystals in convoys of civilian freighters. Further investigation revealed shipments were arriving on Kafrene from the direction of the Unknown Regions before being sent to an unknown destination.

On Kafrene I contacted an intelligence source of mine, Tivik, who'd proved useful in the past. Tivik has always been the nervous sort, but this time he was terrified. He didn't want to meet with me, warning that Imperial spies were everywhere and his communications were being monitored.

When I managed to track down Tivik, he revealed why he was so frightened. He told me that an Imperial cargo pilot named Bodhi Rook had defected the previous day on Jedha. Someone named Galen Erso had convinced Rook to find Saw Gerrera and warn him that the Empire was preparing to test a weapon that used kyber crystals and had enough power to destroy a planet.

Before I could find out more, stormtroopers approached us. They were clearly looking for Tivik. I eliminated the troopers and then neutralized Tivik to prevent him from being taken into Imperial custody. I then returned to Base One at all speed.

SUBJECT: Jyn Erso

AGE: 22

PLACE OF BIRTH: Vallt

RECENT ALIASES: Liana Hallik, Lyra Rallik, Kestrel Dawn, Tanith Ponta, Nari McVee

Jyn Erso was born on Vallt during the Clone Wars. A partial document recovered from an Arakyd Industries data storehouse on Vulpter reveals that her parents, Galen and Lyra Erso, were researching energy creation and storage for Arakyd. We have two other official records of Jyn Erso: a residence permit from Coruscant issued in the first year of the Empire and a visitor's permit for the Outer Rim planet Alpinn, which states that she is three years old.

Our next report of Jyn Erso comes from the Commenor Underground, which briefly coordinated operations with Saw Gerrera's militia nearly a decade ago. Arhul Nemo, a lieutenant in the Commenor Underground, met Gerrera's fighters and reported that his favorite was a twelve-year-old girl named Jyn. Gerrera claimed he'd rescued her from the Empire and raised her as his own.

We aren't sure how Jyn Erso wound up in Gerrera's militia, when she left, or why she did so. After that we have her Imperial arrest records as a street fighter, smuggler, and petty criminal. She drifted from planet to planet, acquiring and discarding fake names, until she was arrested on Corulag and sentenced to a labor camp on Wobani.

PARTIAL LIST OF CRIMINAL WARRANTS:

CRIMINAL WARRANTS

- Forgery of Imperial documents
- Aggravated assault against
  Imperial personnel
- Escape from custody
- Resisting arrest
- Shipjacking
- Impersonation of
  an Imperial official
- Forgery of Imperial documents
- Possession of unsanctioned weapons
- Unlawful contact with undesirables
- Petty theft
- Creating a public nuisance
- Disorderly conduct

IMAGE CELL 00013

(FOR MORE INFORMATION SEE CRACKEN/ANDOR PROG40062
AND IMPERIAL ARREST ADDENDUM 41.3711.)

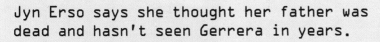

☐
■ Jyn Erso says she thought her father was
☐ dead and hasn't seen Gerrera in years.

◁ ◁ MISSION BRIEF:

LIBERATION OF ERSO

After receiving Capt. Andor's report from Kafrene, Rebel Intelligence immediately analyzed our own files and information captured from Imperial databases.

We concluded that the man who encouraged Bodhi Rook to defect was indeed Galen Erso, a scientist who did work for the Republic and Empire years ago in the field of energy enhancement. Our analysis also turned up information about Jyn Erso, Galen Erso's daughter and a former fighter for Saw Gerrera (see related file). We agreed that Jyn Erso was an essential source: she could identify Galen Erso and might know more about his research.

We located arrest records for Jyn Erso and discovered that she was being held in a labor camp on Wobani under the alias Liana Hallik. Once this information was verified, Gen. Draven approved the formation of a rapid-response team of rebel marines, led by **SGT. MELSHI**.

Sgt. Melshi's team timed its arrival on Wobani for when Erso would be part of a work detail's convoy, then moved to extract her. The operation went smoothly: Jyn Erso's identity was verified and she was freed.

Erso responded by trying to assault her rescuers and escape, but was stopped by K-2SO and taken into rebel custody.

IMAGE CELL 00014

IMAGE CELL 00015

The commander allowed me
to be in the briefing
room at Base One when Jyn
Erso was brought before
her and the rest of the
rebel high command. Erso
is young. Looking at
her, you'd never think
she'd be able to fight
her way past veteran
rebel troops, though Sgt.
Melshi assured me that's
what happened when our
marines broke her out of
an Imperial prison.

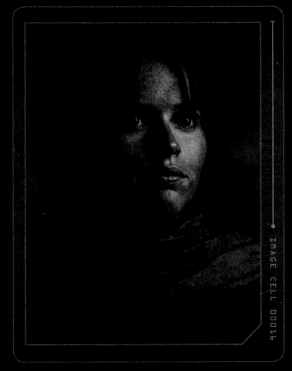

Jyn Erso

Perhaps that's why she
was kept in binders as
Gen. Draven read through
a list of charges for which she'd been arrested. She
waited quietly as he read them, but I was watching Mon
Mothma, and I noticed that the commander was studying
Erso's face. Later, when this is all over, I'll ask the
commander for an interview. I hope she'll share what she
was thinking in those moments.

When they asked Erso
if Galen Erso was her
father, she said he was
but added that she'd
spent sixteen years
assuming he was dead.
When they asked about
Saw Gerrera, she said
she hadn't seen him
in years.

The commander told
Erso that by helping
us she'd get a fresh
start, but she seemed
indifferent to our
cause, telling the room that
she's never had the "luxury"
of political opinions. I
found that curious, because
I know she once served as a
fighter for Gerrera. Perhaps
he did something that made
her reject our movement. She
wouldn't be the first to
think Gerrera's actions have
given our cause a bad name.

Then again, it is clear
she is no friend of the
Empire. So who is she
instead? I don't think any
of us know that yet.

Galen Erso

IMAGE CELL 00017

Saw Gerrera

GEN. DRAVEN TO COMMANDER MOTHMA

Commander, I object in the strongest possible terms to allowing Jyn Erso to join the Operation Fracture team for its mission to Jedha.

IMAGE CELL 00018

JYN ERSO is both a petty criminal and a possible rebel deserter. Her arrest record speaks for itself. When Sgt. Melshi's forces freed her from Wobani—at great risk to themselves—she showed no gratitude but immediately began to fight them. I've only observed her for a few minutes, but during that time she has been defiant, uncooperative, and rude. And you are now proposing that we put her back in contact with Saw Gerrera, a man who has disgraced the rebel cause many times.

Like Gerrera, Jyn Erso is the kind of person who has given our rebel movement a terrible name. She has no loyalty to any person or cause except herself. She should have been left in jail. I urge you to reconsider.

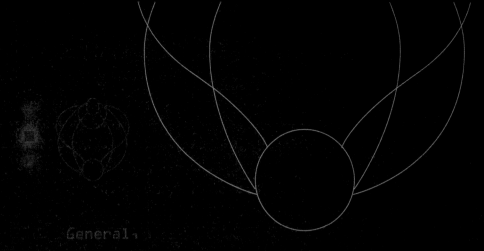

General,

I've read your message about Jyn Erso, and as
always I appreciate your thoughts and your passion
for our cause.

I understand she is rude and defiant—I saw that up
close—and I share your feelings about Saw Gerrera.

But two things:

First, Jyn Erso gives us our only chance to identify
Galen Erso and persuade him to testify in the
Senate about the Emperor's secret weapons program.
Without her, we are lost in the dark, hoping to
find a mysterious weapon that might be the end of
our fight for freedom.

Second, I have reviewed her arrest records and
find no evidence that she's attacked civilians or
tried to swindle them. The targets of her crimes
have always been Imperial officials or fellow
members of the galactic underworld.

From Capt. Andor to Hera Syndulla, many of our
best soldiers and agents were missing something
in their lives until the rebel movement gave
them a sense of purpose and a feeling that they
belonged. Without that, they might have spent
their lives as lost as Jyn Erso has been.

I believe she deserves a second chance, as we all do.

Mon Mothma

MISSION OVERVIEW

GEN. DRAVEN TO CAPT. ANDOR

Commander, here are Capt. Andor's orders as issued.

YOUR PRIMARY MISSION OBJECTIVES:

FIRST PHASE

1. Escort Jyn Erso to Jedha, with K-2SO to secure her cooperation if necessary. Once on Jedha, accompany Erso to the Holy City.

2. Make contact with Saw Gerrera's militia, with Erso's cooperation if possible. Beware of Imperial forces that may be expecting contact between Gerrera and another rebel cell.

3. Find the Imperial defector identified as Bodhi Rook (see related file) and either extract him from Jedha aboard a U-wing or discover what information he has about the Imperial weapons test. We believe Rook will be found with Gerrera's fighters.

4. Discover whereabouts of Galen Erso from Rook and/ or Gerrera. Take any and all measures necessary to discover Erso's location. Once this mission objective is complete, contact Base One for additional orders. If it's impossible to contact us, proceed with the mission's second phase.

INCOMING
0054 1000

SECOND PHASE

5. Identify Galen Erso by having Jyn Erso verify that he is her father. If that is no longer possible, identification can be made by Bodhi Rook or by using evidence from Imperial personnel/datafiles.

6. Extract Galen Erso and return him to Base One at all speed, along with any research about the weapon that you can obtain. Keep him alive at all costs. The commander wants him to testify before the Senate about the Imperial weapon.

YOUR SECONDARY MISSION OBJECTIVES:

1. Observe Imperial mining operations and transportation of kyber crystals on Jedha to gather information for possible rebel sabotage missions.

2. Gather information about Gerrera's supporters, operations, and facilities, and observe how the local population on JEDHA regards his rebel movement.

3. Gather any and all intelligence about the Imperial weapons test for further analysis at Base One.

EXT. OCCUPIED CITY:——

Initial Intel

OCCUPIED TERRITORY

MAIN BREACH
/CITY WALL

IMPERIAL
P.O.W.

TEMPLE OF PROJEMA

DESERT DEFENCE GRC GUNS

REFUGEE CONVOY THROUGH
PRIMARY GATE/CHECKPOINT
CITY WALL /DESERT DEFENCE

REFUGEE CAMP

FORMER KAIBURR
REFINERY

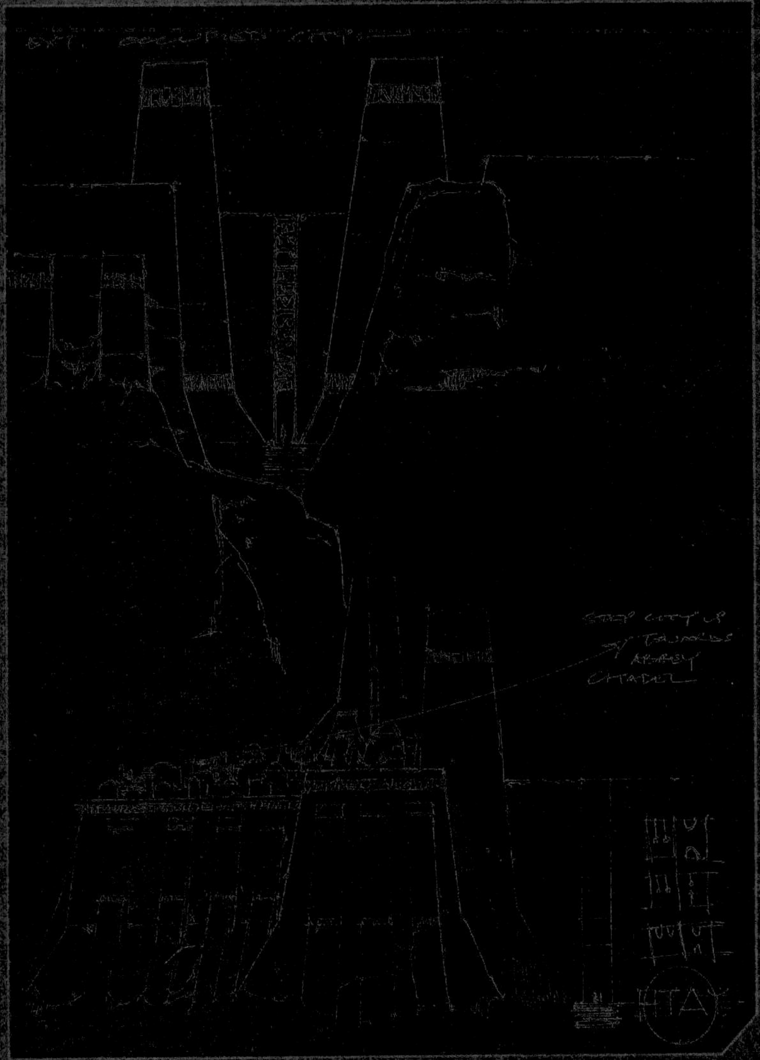

N.B. FORMER KAIBURR CRYSTAL
MINING COLONY AND ANCIENT
CAPITAL/SEAT OF THE JEDI
ORDER (OVER 3000 YEARS OLD).

. CITY IS BUILT INTO AND UP OUT
OF THE MINE /QUARRY ITSELF.

EXT. OCCUPIED CITY

STEP CITY UP
TOWARDS
ARMORY
CITADEL

CAPT. CASSIAN ANDOR

Capable fighter; unshakably loyal to rebel cause

Learned of Erso message from intelligence contact

Has a wide range of skills that allows him to improvise as needed

JYN ERSO

Daughter of Galen Erso and former fighter for Saw Gerrera

Needed to gain access to Gerrera and identify Galen Erso

Security risk due to background as petty criminal

K-2SO

Reprogrammed Imperial enforcer droid

Has an appearance ideal for infiltrating Imperial facilities

Can prevent Jyn Erso from endangering mission

SAW GERRERA

Rebel leader on Jedha; former associate of Jyn Erso

Thought to be the intended recipient of the Erso message

May assist our mission or try to prevent its success

BODHI ROOK

Imperial defector born on Jedha; served Empire as cargo pilot

Connections with Galen Erso and Saw Gerrera unclear

Current location unknown

GALEN ERSO

Imperial research scientist we believe is key to weapons project

Father of Jyn Erso; connection with Saw Gerrera unclear

Mission objective to return him to Base One for further questioning

CAPT. CASSIAN ANDOR

 GEN. DRAVEN TO COMMANDER MOTHMA

Commander, I strongly support the assignment of Capt. Andor to Operation Fracture.

Capt. Andor is one of the most capable agents within Rebel Intelligence. He is a valuable fighter on the battlefield, able to handle missions ranging from reconnaissance and infiltration to assassination and sabotage. This makes him ideal for Operation Fracture, as we simply don't know what our team will find on Jedha. Whatever the mission demands, Capt. Andor will be able to accomplish it.

CAPT. ANDOR is also skilled at gathering information and figuring out what it means, without having to report back to base for assistance or instruction. He has made contacts on many Imperial-held worlds and has repeatedly brought back information that's proved valuable to us. His learning of the Erso message on Kafrene is just the latest example of this.

I trust Capt. Andor to make contact with Saw Gerrera on Jedha and retrieve the information contained in the Erso message. He will do whatever it takes to accomplish this goal. I also trust him to figure out what he should do next. Capt. Andor has worked with the rebels since he was a child. It is no exaggeration to say that we are his family. He is absolutely loyal to the rebel cause and will do whatever he must to achieve our goals.

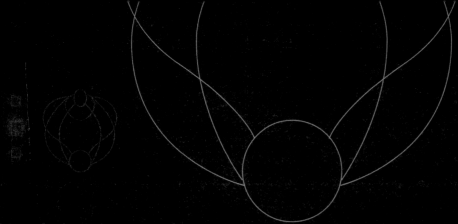

General,

Your request to assign Capt. Andor to Operation Fracture is approved.

I have never doubted Capt. Andor's abilities or his dedication to the rebel movement. He is truly one of our best and brightest, and I trust his judgment on this mission.

I am concerned about him, however. I understand that for our rebel movement to survive, brave men and women must do terrible things that we'd rather not talk about. But what happens to those men and women afterward? Are we doing enough to help them live with what they've had to do? Do we encourage them when they feel guilty? Comfort them when they can't sleep? And do we notice when they stop feeling guilty? When they no longer lose sleep?

Capt. Andor has been a rebel fighter his entire life. You say this with pride, and I'm sure he would, too. But it worries me. If we succeed and overthrow the Empire, what kind of life will someone like Capt. Andor have?

Mon Mothma

K-2SO is a KX-model enforcer droid who has been reprogrammed
to serve our cause. While his size and appearance have
alarmed some rebel personnel, he has proved valuable on
many missions.

Arakyd Industries created the KX line to provide Imperial
facilities with more efficient security. Unlike most
fourth-degree droids, the KX model was programmed to
speak and interact with organic beings, though it isn't
particularly good at doing so when compared with a
protocol droid. KX droids can handle a range of tasks,
from communicating with superiors and escorting visitors
to defending key personnel and neutralizing targets.

KX droids have built-in behavioral inhibitors and fail-
safes in their memory banks; K-2SO may be the only example
of one that's been successfully reprogrammed. This makes
him ideal for infiltrating bases or prisons. Imperial
personnel are unlikely to be surprised by his presence
even in normally restricted areas.

IMAGE CELL 00026

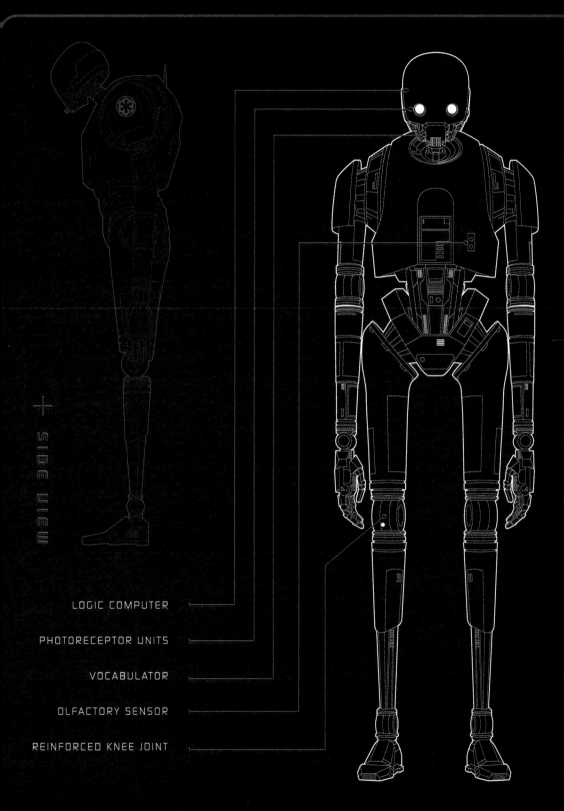

LOGIC COMPUTER

PHOTORECEPTOR UNITS

VOCABULATOR

OLFACTORY SENSOR

REINFORCED KNEE JOINT

SAW GERRERA

GEN. CRACKEN TO COMMANDER MOTHMA

Why did Galen Erso send his message about the Empire's weapons test to Jedha?

We must consider the possibility that Erso wanted his message to reach **SAW GERRERA** personally.

Galen Erso's daughter, Jyn (see related file), was part of Gerrera's militia during her youth. That suggests an earlier connection between Gerrera and Galen Erso, though we don't know what it is.

But I'm sure you remember, Commander, that Gerrera believed the Empire was creating an incredibly powerful weapon somewhere in the galaxy. Perhaps he was right—or at least on the right track—and Galen Erso reached out to him because he knew Gerrera would believe his warning.

I personally believe Erso's message is real, Commander. But if Gerrera has learned of the Imperial weapons test, that's very dangerous.

His years of fighting the Empire have left him unstable, so consumed with hatred for the Empire that he has done more damage than good to the rebel cause. Since retreating to Jedha, Gerrera has done our movement relatively little harm.

But I fear what he will do when he receives Erso's message. He is likely to foolishly lash out, as he has done ever since his days as a young resistance fighter on Onderon.

IMAGE CELL 00031

Saw Gerrera's fatal flaw as a leader is he's never understood that most people value peace and order even more than freedom. Our rebel cause gains support when people believe we can make them safe and free from the Empire's tyranny. It loses support when people believe we will replace the Empire's order with chaos and danger.

GALEN ERSO

GEN. CRACKEN TO COMMANDER MOTHMA

Who is Galen Erso? We know he is a gifted mathematician and scientist, and that the Empire considers him extremely important to its weapons program. If we can rescue him from Imperial service, perhaps we can stop whatever this test is.

But why did Erso send Bodhi Rook to Jedha with a warning about the weapons test? Has something changed Erso's mind about working for the Empire? Is he working against his will? We also don't know what Erso's connection is with Saw Gerrera.

This partial document was retrieved from an Arakyd Industries facility on Vulpter. Document information indicates it was created during the CLONE WARS:

VALLT EXPERIMENTAL FUSION FACILITY EMPLOYMENT ROSTER

EMPLOYEE: Erso, Galen
AGE: 43
BIRTH WORLD: Grange
RESOURCE ID: 455C-1228-75-6ZZ-2

RELEVANT EDUCATION/EMPLOYMENT: Rocantor Sector Futures Program; Brentaal Futures Program; Republic Ministry of Energy (internship); Humbarine Academy of Advanced Studies; Obroa-skai College (teaching fellow); Republic Sienar EnerCo (visiting scholar); Denon Laboratories (professor); Institute of Applied Science (Coruscant)

RELEVANT SPECIALTIES: applied mathematics, theoretical physics, energy generation and enhancement, materials science, crystallography

IMAGE CELL 00033

Either the Republic or the Empire classified or erased *all* references to Erso's scientific research and his personal life, but Arakyd used Republic citizen identification numbers for its employee records—as did the early Empire.

By searching for Galen Erso's citizen identification number, we confirmed his birth on Grange and much of the above information. We also discovered something else: soon after the end of the Clone Wars, Erso was named research director for the B'ANKORA division of an Imperial program called Project Celestial Power and took the Official Secrets Oath.

See our file on Director Krennic for more on Project Celestial Power. The fact that Krennic and Erso are both connected to this program makes us suspect the Imperial weapons test uses technologies originally developed for Celestial Power. We continue to investigate this potential connection.

The B'ankora are a species granted a refuge on Coruscant 112 years before the end of the Republic and relocated to Parau VI by the Empire. They are now extinct. What does this reference mean?

Bail,

Galen Erso is the key to the Empire's weapon—
I know it.

We MUST see him delivered to the Senate to tell
the galaxy what the Emperor has ordered his
scientists to create. When the people of the
galaxy learn that Palpatine is trying to build
a planet-killer, they will finally understand
that he seeks to rule not through laws and order
but through terror.

I'm convinced if the Senate learns the truth,
it will revolt against Palpatine's leadership
and refuse to believe any more of his lies.

Mon Mothma

GEN. DRAVEN TO COMMANDER MOTHMA

Our intelligence analysts have done excellent work piecing together information about Galen Erso—information the Empire tried very hard to erase.

I'm concerned to learn that Erso is an expert in crystal science and energy generation. That fits with the warning that the Empire's weapon uses kyber crystals. The connection to Krennic disturbs me, as well. Nearly twenty years ago, Galen Erso was skilled enough to be named research director of part of a secret Imperial project. What has he learned since then, and what kind of weapon could the Empire create with that knowledge?

Ma'am, I know you want to see Erso tell the Senate what he knows. But I'm concerned that Erso may know too much for us to take that risk.

IMAGE CELL 00035

AGE: 25
PLACE OF BIRTH: Jedha

IMAGE CELL 00036

According to Capt. Andor's intelligence source, Bodhi Rook defected from the Empire to bring Galen Erso's warning about the weapons test to Jedha.

His whereabouts are now unknown. We do not believe Rook has been recaptured by the Empire. Communications traffic on Jedha spiked soon after the date of his defection and has not returned to normal levels. Our sources on Jedha have also reported increased security around transports leaving the moon.

As Rook is native to Jedha, he may be in hiding. It's also possible that Saw Gerrera's forces are sheltering Rook. We simply do not know; hopefully, Operation Fracture can supply answers.

Our slicers have managed to access Rook's service records. Unfortunately, his active service record is classified and encrypted. We don't know where he was assigned, only basic information from his enlistment and training.

Local information on Jedha reveals two legal violations for Rook— one for unlawful wagering on sporting events, the other for unsafe operation of an airspeeder. Both came when he was a juvenile; in each case he was fined and put on probation. Neither violation was serious enough to prevent him from being accepted for Imperial pilot training.

Rook entered the Terrabe Sector Service Academy seven years ago, chose flight training, and graduated from a two-year program with average grades. His marks weren't high enough for a starfighter academy. One instructor noted that he was skilled but seemed to get nervous during flight tests. He remained at the service academy, where he spent two more years in flight training. At the end of that period, he was rated flight ready for handling cargo transports, tenders, and shuttles and granted the rank of ensign.

After that point we can find no mention of Bodhi Rook until Capt. Andor's report. There is nothing in his service record that makes him different from millions of Imperial recruits—except his homeworld of Jedha.

LOCATION BRIEFING: JEDHA

Jedha is a small, chilly desert moon in the Mid Rim on the edge of the galaxy's Unknown Regions. It lies in an area of space that's nearly forgotten today. Jedha was settled thousands of years ago, but shifting stars have erased most hyperspace routes to it and its neighbors.

The ancient history of Jedha is one of myths and legends. No one can tell where fact ends and storytelling begins.

HOLY CITY PILGRIMS

IMAGE CELL 00038

Jedha is one of the oldest worlds associated with the Jedi Order, and some scholars think it is where the Jedi began. The Empire has restricted access to information about Jedha and monitors Holonet conversations about the moon. Fortunately, the Empire can't take away people's memories, and some brave worshippers of the Church of the Force have preserved histories written before the Empire's rise to power.

Believers in many faiths, including ones banned by the Empire, still visit Jedha, paying large amounts of money to guides and lying about their reasons for traveling to the moon. Their hope is to visit the Temple of the Kyber and leave an offering—or just touch its ancient walls while the stormtroopers guarding the site aren't looking. Pilgrims who trust the wrong guides often wind up robbed of their money, thrown into an Imperial detention cell, or both.

In recent years the Empire has begun mining operations on Jedha, leaving large parts of the moon scarred and polluted. Rumor has it the Empire is seeking kyber crystals. Many Jedhans work in the mines, alongside construction droids and aliens seeking a better life.

The ancient Holy City of Jedha is a chaotic labyrinth of narrow streets where pilgrims, miners, water-hawkers, beggars, and Imperial troops all jostle for space. Periodically, the Empire sweeps in to arrest pilgrims or is attacked by Saw Gerrera's militia.

It is difficult to know whom to trust on Jedha. Our team's focus should be on finding Bodhi Rook and any information about Galen Erso and then getting out before the Empire discovers its presence.

Temple of the Kyber as their sacred duty. They continue to perform this duty despite the fact that the Empire has closed the temple down and banned the Guardians as a terrorist organization.

The Guardians work to keep Jedha's pilgrims safe, protecting them from unscrupulous guides and alerting them to danger from stormtroopers or Saw Gerrera's militia. They wear disguises and seek shelter in hidden places within the Holy City, appearing and disappearing quickly and quietly.

Our intelligence agents have discovered one such guardian named CHIRRUT ÎMWE. Îmwe is blind and often disguises himself as one of the many beggars in the Holy City. But don't be fooled by his blindness. Îmwe is an experienced warrior, able to sense the location of opponents and either gracefully escape from danger or close in on his enemies and neutralize them. Whether Îmwe uses the Force or is a master of some other martial art is unknown to us.

IMAGE CELL 00040

Îmwe's companion in the Guardians of the Whills is BAZE MALBUS, a shaggy man who is Îmwe's opposite. Malbus favors energy weapons, and there are conflicting reports that he may have worked as a mercenary. He is wanted on Jedha for conducting hit-and-run attacks on Imperial forces.

The Guardians of the Whills are enemies of the Empire. The Emperor has destroyed the Jedi Order, punished worshippers of the Church of the Force, and stripped the temple of its artifacts.

But that doesn't mean that the Guardians are allies of our rebel movement. Their only allegiance is to the will of the Force—but the Jedi Order is no longer around to help them understand what the Force is telling them. They are left to defend the shell of their temple, and they see both the Empire's forces and Gerrera's fighters as intruders who have brought chaos and fear to the Holy City.

SENATOR JEBEL TO COMMANDER MOTHMA

We must consider the possibility that the Erso message is a trick meant to destroy our rebel movement.

These weapons systems are fantasies, Commander. If the Empire was actually crazy enough to build a superlaser with the power to destroy a planet, it wouldn't work. The first shot would burn out the focusing crystals, melt down the power source, or both.

I believe the Erso message is meant to frighten us into revealing our own intelligence sources or to trick us into thinking our only choice is surrendering to the Emperor.

I urge you not to be fooled, ma'am.

THE EMPIRE

◁ ◁ INTEL BRIEFING: IMPERIAL WEAPONS TEST

Commander, the Empire is preparing a major weapons test that our agents believe will be the largest in Imperial military history. We don't know what form this weapons test will take or where it will take place. But the weapon supposedly has enough power to destroy a planet.

On a recent mission (see related file), Capt. Andor learned from an intelligence source that an Imperial cargo pilot, Bodhi Rook, deserted on Jedha. According to Andor's source, Rook claimed to have proof of the existence of an Imperial planet-killer powered by kyber crystals.

Some of our analysts believe this message is a trick, but I believe the man who encouraged Rook to desert is indeed Galen Erso (see related file). If so, Erso is risking his life by contacting us.

While we have no spies inside Imperial weapons research, our agents say Director Krennic has been traveling with heavy security in recent months, visiting planets deeply involved in Imperial weapons research. We have verified communications between those planets and Eriadu, the homeworld of Governor Tarkin, and Tarkin's flagship, the *EXECUTRIX*.

Everything I have reviewed suggests the weapons test is real, Commander—and a terrible threat to us all.

GEN. DODONNA TO COMMANDER MOTHMA

What is the weapons platform that the Empire plans to test?

Jan Dodonna

We simply don't know enough to answer this question, but we have long suspected that the Empire has spent years seizing kyber crystals and transporting them to weapons labs—and, it's rumored, taking them to secret bases in the Unknown Regions.

We know little about kyber crystals, because the Jedi Order worked to keep knowledge of them secret. But to put it simply, they focus energy and amplify its intensity. That once made them ideal for use in Jedi lightsabers; now it makes them ideal for use in laser weapons.

For nearly two decades, Imperials have mined deposits of kyber crystals under heavy security. But to our puzzlement, we haven't seen new weapons systems that use these crystals.

Perhaps the Empire has figured out how to mount a planet-killing superlaser on a warship. But to supply power for a superlaser, a capital ship would have to be at least the size of a *Mandator*-class Dreadnaught—and even then, the weapon wouldn't be powerful enough to destroy a planet.

We know the Empire has researched such weapons—just like the Republic and the Separatists did during the Clone Wars. And we continue to investigate rumors that Imperial researchers have tried to scale up the industrial superlasers used in Geonosian factories. Saw Gerrera, for one, was certain this was the reason the Empire sterilized the surface of Geonosis.

An alternative would be to build a superlaser on the surface of a planet or moon. But a "battle moon" wouldn't be able to move on its own, so it couldn't threaten planets in other star systems. Some researchers have proposed weapons that could fire through hyperspace, but so far such weapons are merely theoretical.

Perhaps the Empire is working on a system for coordinating attacks by many warships at once. Last month our agents learned of the existence of a weapons program code-named Cluster Prism. But I don't know why such a system would require large numbers of kyber crystals.

Mon Mothma

We simply don't know enough to draw conclusions, Commander. It's urgent that our team discovers if Erso gave any other information to Rook and finds Erso himself to learn more.

IMAGE CELL 00046

DIRECTOR ORSON KRENNIC

ORSON KRENNIC is the Empire's director of advanced weapons research. But despite our agents' best efforts, we know frustratingly little about his work for the Empire.

We do know that Krennic is ruthless about security. Scientists and researchers who work for his department have their identities deleted from public databases. Their families are considered "heroes of the Empire," which is a fancy name for well-treated prisoners. These scientists are watched wherever they go and never talk about their work. And a suspicious number of those who retire from Krennic's labs soon disappear.

But it would be a mistake to assume the scientists who work for Krennic hate him. Many of Krennic's scientists are fiercely loyal to him and truly believe in the work they're doing for the Empire.

Most of Krennic's personal information has been classified or erased, and we don't know what happened to Krennic's parents.

We do know that Krennic joined the Corps of Engineers, working in the design regiment. He wound up supervising the construction of many government headquarters on Coruscant, including military facilities. He was selected to join the Republic's Strategic Advisory Cell as part of the Special Weapons Group.

The Special Weapons Group's job was to research advanced weapons, test them, and recommend them for use by the Grand Army of the Republic and the Republic Navy. The Separatists had an experimental weapons program of their own, and an arms race between the two sides led to advances in targeting accuracy, shield generation, hull armor, and energy production.

Most documents from this period are classified, but we know Krennic was never considered a great mathematician or scientist. Instead, he was an excellent manager, able to keep track of what the scientists were working on and make sure projects stayed on schedule.

After the Republic became the Empire, we found references connecting Krennic to another project, Celestial Power (see Galen Erso's file). The few mentions of Celestial Power describe it as a research project intended to provide sustainable energy for remote planets or planets damaged during the Clone Wars.

Given Krennic's later career, we suspect that Celestial Power was either a code name for a military research program or a civilian program whose discoveries could also be used for military purposes. While the Empire has brought badly needed energy to many worlds, particularly in the Outer Rim, we could find no mention of Celestial Power in connection with any of those efforts. It is possible that Celestial Power is somehow connected to the Empire's weapons test.

Based on what we know of Krennic, we can say that like Governor Tarkin he believes in an Empire based on power. We suspect that Krennic wants to help make the Empire powerful enough to rule the entire galaxy. Nothing else matters to him—not the lives of scientists who want a quiet retirement after years of service or the ambitions of rivals or the objections of the Senate.

We believe Krennic will eliminate anyone who gets in his way.

▷ ▷ REBEL INTELLIGENCE BRIEFING:

GOVERNOR TARKIN

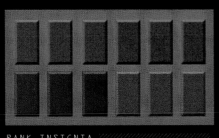

RANK INSIGNIA

Wilhuff Tarkin is governor of the Outer Rim Territories, an important position in the Empire. Only the Emperor himself has more influence over Imperial policy or has done more to bring planets under Imperial rule.

Born on the Outer Rim world of Eriadu, Tarkin began his career fighting pirates with Eriadu's Outland Regions Security Forces. While at the Sullust Sector Spacefarers Academy, he became friendly with Palpatine, who was Naboo's senator at the time. Palpatine helped Tarkin get an appointment with the Judicial Department and encouraged him to become Eriadu's governor. Tarkin then joined the newly created Republic Navy and rose rapidly through the ranks, becoming an admiral.

Tarkin served on various military tribunals, consulting with Palpatine on intelligence matters and supervising secret operations. Palpatine then named Tarkin as one of twenty moffs in his new Empire and made him the first of his new GRAND MOFFS.

As the Empire grew in power, Tarkin was also the most important thinker behind a new philosophy of Imperial rule, one that became known as the Tarkin doctrine.

Tarkin thinks that it isn't enough for the Imperial military to be strong. It must also be *feared.* And it won't be feared unless it uses its military power and lets the galaxy see the results. The greater the power used by the Empire to defeat its opponents, the less likely that other opponents will defy it. Or so Tarkin believes.

Commander, this psychological profile of Tarkin is a useful look at the man and his beliefs.

Here's what it's missing: our intelligence analysts suspect Tarkin is still performing other duties for the Emperor, just as he did as a Republic officer. We don't know what these missions might be. They have been kept secret from the Senate.

Tarkin certainly knows about the weapons test and the program that created it. Besides his importance in the Imperial hierarchy, we've monitored communications between Krennic and Tarkin's homeworld of Eriadu, as well as points in the Outer Rim. And the rumors about this new weapon's power would fit perfectly with the Tarkin doctrine. Tarkin believes fear can ensure peace, and if anyone could convince the Emperor to spend trillions of credits on a weapon powerful enough to destroy a planet, it's Wilhuff Tarkin.

This leads me to another danger we must consider: we don't know enough about Tarkin's ambitions.

He certainly appears loyal to the Emperor, but is he? Galactic history is full of generals and admirals who supported political leaders but then turned on them and seized power for themselves.

We are worried that the Emperor will use this new weapon against his enemies, and we should be. But we also need to worry that Tarkin—or some other high-ranking Imperial officer—might use this new weapon on his own. A civil war between Imperial forces would be catastrophic, leading to trillions of deaths.

DARTH VADER

DARTH VADER is the Emperor's enforcer and an extension of his will. Palpatine uses this armored warrior to punish rebellious planets, hunt down dangerous fugitives, and discover potential threats to the Emperor's power.

Vader has served alongside Governor Tarkin and other Imperials who we suspect are involved with the weapons program and the secret test. The Emperor relies on Vader to keep an eye on ambitious officers who might be tempted by power, warning him of any sign of disloyalty. Vader's mere presence is a reminder to those officers that the Emperor is watching them.

The threat to our agents is more direct. Vader is an ace pilot, is fearless and deadly in hand-to-hand combat, and has an uncanny knack for finding double agents and hidden operatives. Any rebel agents sent on this mission should be aware of the possibility that Vader will be present, seeking to protect the Empire's weapons program. He will certainly be alert to any attempt to spy on this work or sabotage it.

If our agents spot Vader, they should remember that there is no servant of the Empire more dangerous than this mysterious warrior. If they see him, they are in MORTAL PERIL.

For more on Vader see Bail
Organa memo code-named
Mirrorbright—my eyes only.

STORMTROOPER UNITS

LT. SEFLA TO GEN. DRAVEN

IMAGE CELL 00052

Our team can expect to encounter both regular stormtrooper units and specialized units on Jedha. The moon's been kept under heavy security for a number of reasons: to restrict access to the Temple of the Kyber, to protect the Empire's mining operations, and to battle Saw Gerrera's rebels.

The Empire considers Jedha a hazardous assignment, and stormtrooper units there will be familiar with its terrain and the locals. Gen. Cracken's analysts are seeking information about Imperial deployments to determine if our team will encounter troops familiar with local conditions or newcomers to the moon.

Nonstandard units on Jedha may include scout troopers on speeder bikes and tank troopers accompanying TX-225A Occupier tanks. Those units typically wear lighter armor to give them improved mobility in cramped urban settings and are specially trained for reconnaissance and skirmish operations.

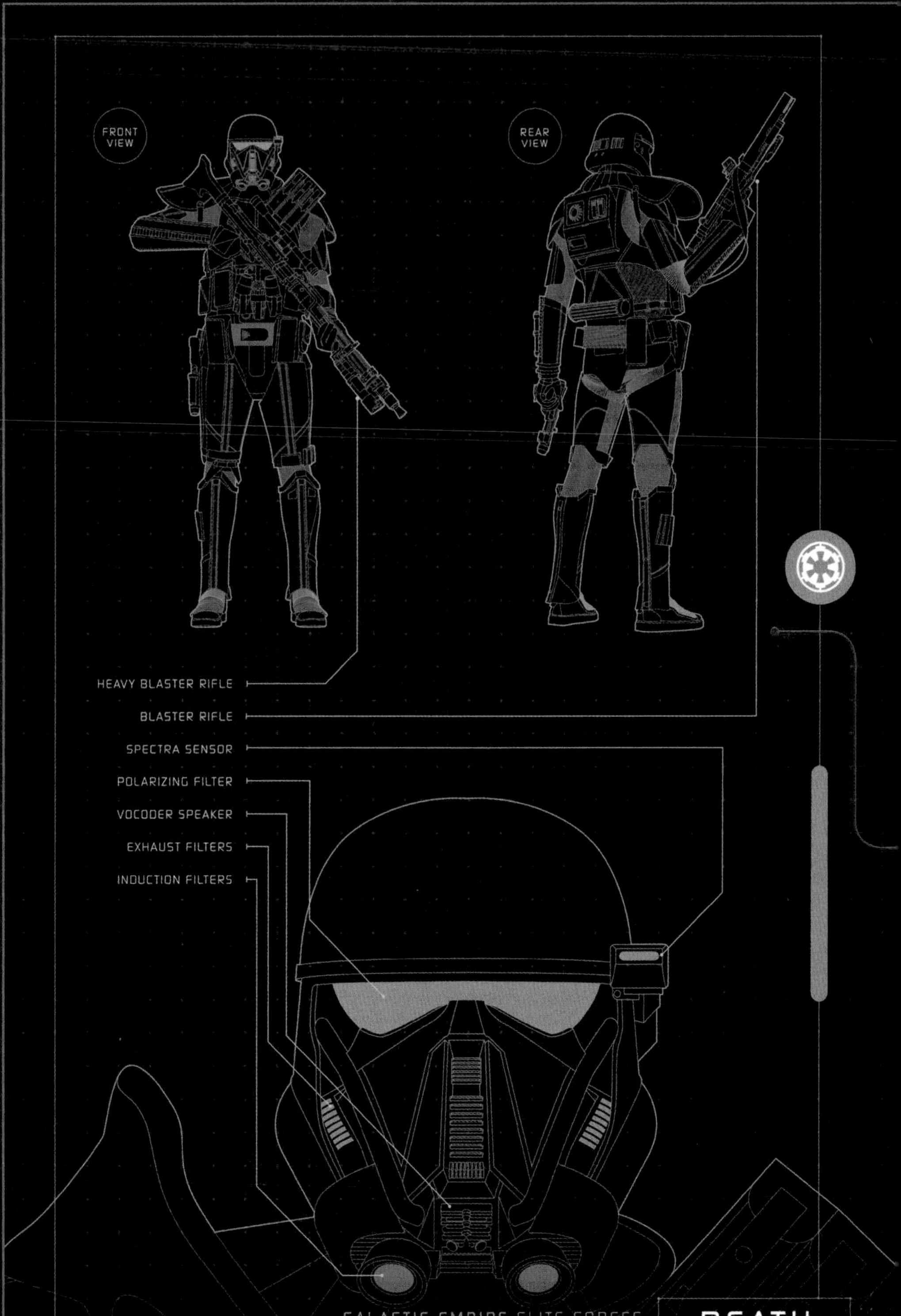
FRONT VIEW
REAR VIEW
HEAVY BLASTER RIFLE
BLASTER RIFLE
SPECTRA SENSOR
POLARIZING FILTER
VOCODER SPEAKER
EXHAUST FILTERS
INDUCTION FILTERS

GALACTIC EMPIRE ELITE FORCES

DEATH

The most dangerous units our team may face are death troopers—elite stormtroopers that are part of Imperial Intelligence. These soldiers serve as bodyguards for top officers within the Imperial military hierarchy, often as part of protection squadrons. According to intelligence, Director Krennic never travels without a squadron of these troopers and seems to consider them his personal guard.

Few Imperial civilians ever see a death trooper. They protect key Imperial facilities and specialize in commando missions, relying on stealth, intelligence, and force to make lightning-quick assaults. They're careful to cover their tracks, too, leaving little trace of their targets or tactics once a mission is complete.

⊙ **DEATH TROOPERS** train as snipers, practice unarmed combat, and are taught to use heavy weapons. We do not know if such training is standard for all death troopers or if certain units or individual troopers are chosen to specialize. We also don't know if death trooper units always work independently or are rotated in and out of the larger Stormtrooper Corps.

But we do know this: our operatives should expect to encounter death troopers defending Krennic and his project. When they do, they should remember these elite troops are lethal opponents.

IMPERIAL MILITARY UNITS

LT. SEFLA TO GEN. DRAVEN

General, our team on Jedha will find itself in an ancient city with narrow streets and crowded plazas and marketplaces. This will prevent Imperial troops from using their heavier vehicles in combat. Jedha's dense buildings will also make it difficult for TIE fighters to find targets and zero in on them. On the other hand, the crowded conditions will also hamper our own forces' movements, and the locals are likely to panic if fighting breaks out, leading to chaos.

Here are some of the vehicles I'd expect our forces to encounter:

ROTHANA HEAVY ENGINEERING TX-225 COMBAT ASSAULT TANK: The Empire relies on these tanks as its principal heavy vehicle for both peacekeeping operations and offensive missions. These "Occupier" tanks have proven effective on many rebellious worlds but face disadvantages on Jedha. The city's narrow streets limit tanks' mobility, and commanders have difficulty spotting threats in Jedha's crowds. Still, tanks are the most dangerous Imperial vehicle our team is likely to face. Their weapons pack a serious punch, and the Empire won't hesitate to use them even if it means civilian casualties or damage to surrounding buildings.

IMAGE CELL 00057

IMAGE CELL 00057

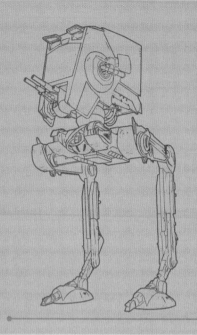

KUAT DRIVE YARDS ALL-TERRAIN SCOUT TRANSPORT (AT-ST):

The Empire has deployed a number of AT-STs on Jedha, but these two-legged vehicles have been rarely seen outside of Imperial bases. They face the same disadvantages as tanks in the narrow streets, and visibility is even worse for their pilots. If our team steers clear of these walkers, they should be able to avoid trouble from them.

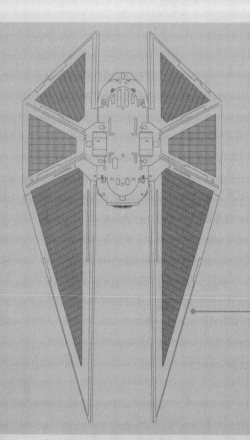

TIE STRIKER:
These variant TIE fighters are more streamlined than the standard model, making them faster in atmospheric flight. Their weapons can level buildings and cause mass casualties, and they fly so quickly that they'll be almost impossible to target with handheld weapons. Our team members should avoid engaging these fighters.

Should our team's mission take it outside of the city, it may encounter other Imperial vehicles. AT-STs are commonly used to defend the Empire's mining operations on Jedha, and those may be backed up by a handful of All-Terrain Armored Transports (AT-ATs) or All-Terrain Armored Cargo Transports (AT-ACTs). Away from urban areas, conventional TIE fighters will also fly in support of TIE strikers.

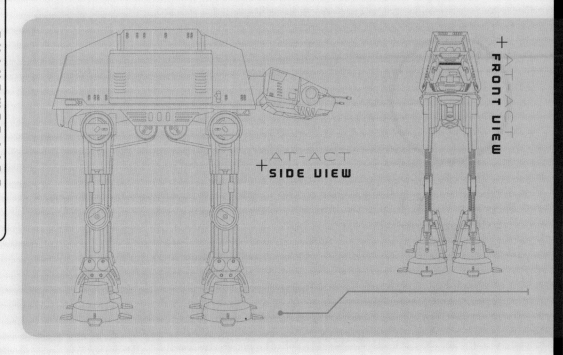

+ AT-ACT
SIDE VIEW

+ AT-ACT
FRONT VIEW

If our team's mission requires it to face these heavier Imperial vehicles, my recommendation is that they join forces with Saw Gerrera's fighters. I know that won't be a popular option, General, but there's no way around it.

READINESS REPORT:

REBEL MILITARY ASSETS

 GEN. DRAVEN TO COMMANDER MOTHMA

Base One will stand ready to support Operation Fracture depending on what happens on Jedha.

Lt. Sefla will be standing by with a full platoon of Special Forces marines, ready to go on our word to any point in the galaxy. We will rotate duty shifts within the platoon so that two squads are combat-ready at any time and two others can be prepped for departure within the hour.

Weapons and gear will be ready for immediate departure, with a **U-WING** and pilot kept hot.

Lt. Sefla has been briefed on Operation Fracture and several potential follow-up missions. His squads will include Pathfinders, urban combat specialists, techs, infiltrators, and heavy weapons specialists, as well as regular SpecForce troopers. Lt. Sefla will brief squad leaders on their way to whatever destination we give them.

We'll be ready, ma'am.

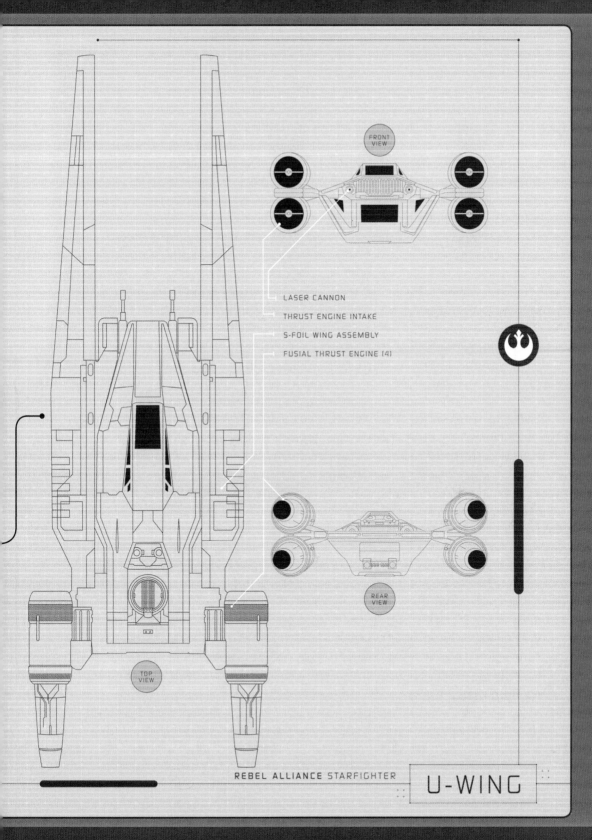

FRONT
VIEW

LASER CANNON

THRUST ENGINE INTAKE

S-FOIL WING ASSEMBLY

FUSIAL THRUST ENGINE (4)

REAR
VIEW

TOP
VIEW

REBEL ALLIANCE STARFIGHTER

U-WING

STARFIGHTERS AND PILOTS

ADMIRAL RADDUS TO COMMANDER MOTHMA

Our starfighter squadrons, U-wings, and heavier fleet units are prepared to support Capt. Andor's mission.

The most likely scenario is an extraction assignment featuring **U-WINGS**. Blue Squadron is at full strength and prepared for duty. Our starfighter ranks have been returned to maximum readiness after recent losses.

The expanded Blue Squadron of X-wing and Y-wing fighters also stands ready. Red Squadron's twelve X-wings and their pilots are flight ready as does Green Squadron.

Nine of Gold Squadron's twelve Y-wings are currently spaceworthy, and maintenance crews are working overtime to return the last three to green flight status. We are transferring ordnance from the rebel fleet to make sure Gold Squadron is properly outfitted for a bombing run, should one prove necessary.

In case reinforcements are needed, allied rebel movements, including the Tierfon Yellow Aces, have been alerted and stand ready to supply starfighters and pilots from their own squadrons.

I am confident we can support whatever Operation Fracture requires.

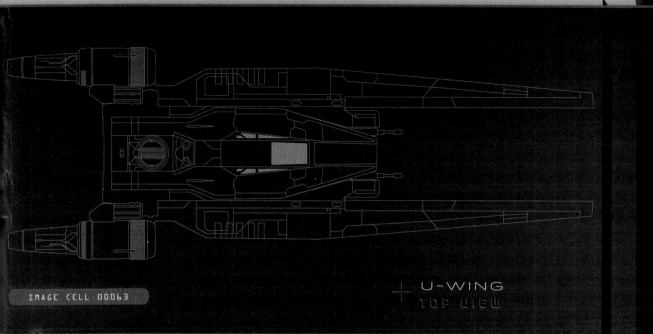

U-WING
TOP VIEW

▷ ▷   RI 592-B1 CONTACT REPORT:

UNKNOWN
CONSTRUCT

LOCATION: COORDINATES
-340.11, -79.72, 1.067-
STANDARD GALACTIC GRID
H-10

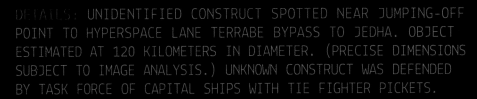

This just came in.
You need to see it, Commander.

⬛ U R G E N T

DETAILS: UNIDENTIFIED CONSTRUCT SPOTTED NEAR JUMPING-OFF
POINT TO HYPERSPACE LANE TERRABE BYPASS TO JEDHA. OBJECT
ESTIMATED AT 120 KILOMETERS IN DIAMETER. (PRECISE DIMENSIONS
SUBJECT TO IMAGE ANALYSIS.) UNKNOWN CONSTRUCT WAS DEFENDED
BY TASK FORCE OF CAPITAL SHIPS WITH TIE FIGHTER PICKETS.

ACTION: PILOT DESIGNATED FAR NEEDLE THETA BROKE OFF CONTACT
TO AVOID CAPTURE AND LOSS OF INTELLIGENCE DATA. IMAGE IS BEING
ENHANCED AND ANALYZED.

▷   **That dish could be a massive, long-range signal-gathering apparatus.** ⬛

▷   OR IT COULD BE A WEAPONS ARRAY. IS IT POSSIBLE THE EMPIRE
HAS SUCCEEDED IN ARTIFICIALLY ARMORING A MOON? ⬛

▷   It's worse than we feared:

That's no moon.

Now more than ever we need Operation Fracture to succeed.

May the Force be with us all. ⬛